I0787940

OCEAN OCEAN

Paul Xylinides

Xylinides Press

Hardcover ISBN 978-0-9919521-4-4
Paperback ISBN 978-0-9919521-6-8
Ebook ISBN 978-0-9919521-5-1

Fiction

Printed in the United States of America

To David who mentored and Gabrielle who inspired

CONTENTS

Wave, Wave, Wave

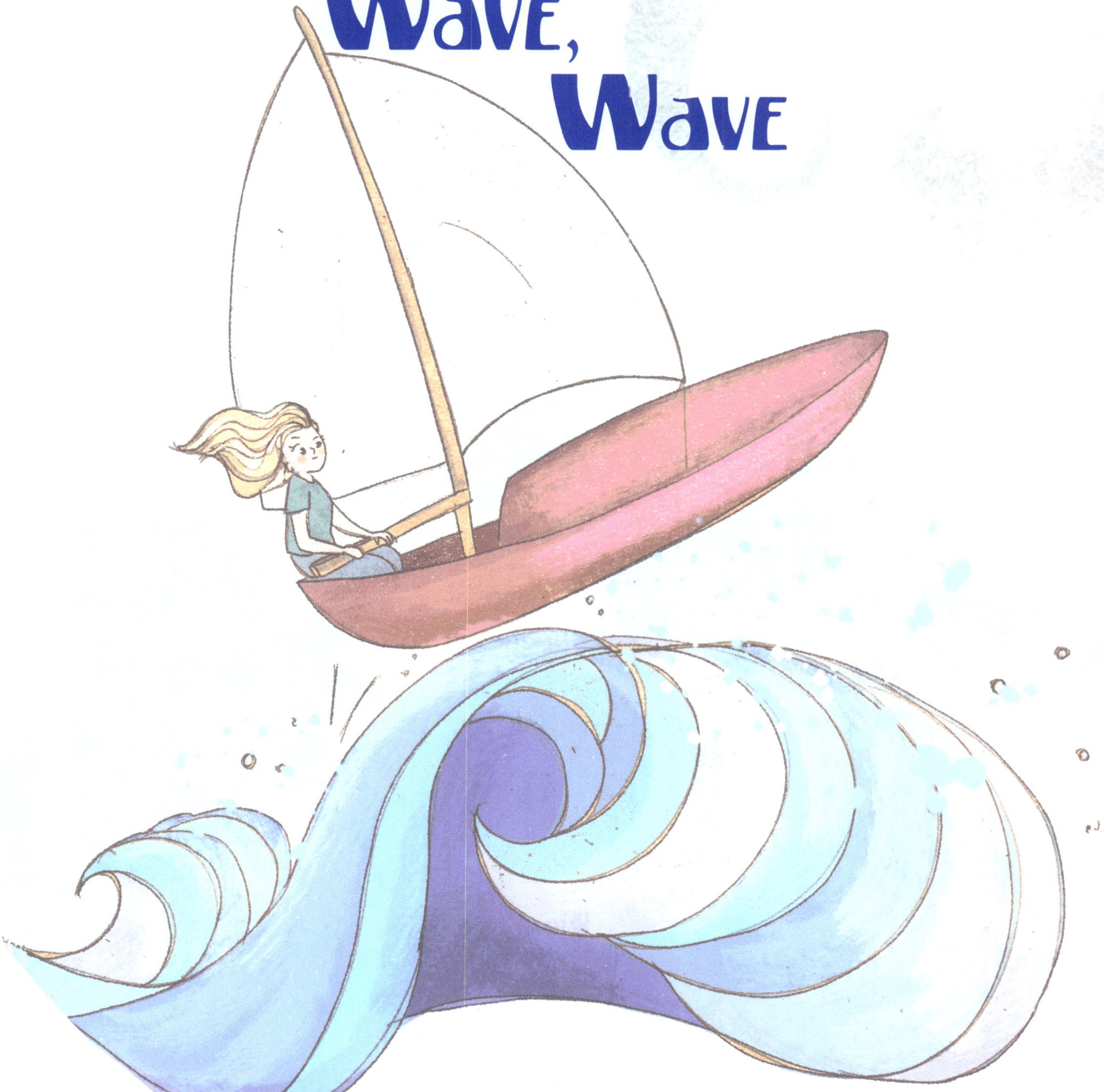

ave lifted Boat higher and higher and deposited it on the cliff.

"Well done! Now go back from where you came!"

Wave plunged down the cliff face into the waves of the waiting sea.

It wasn't a large boat, but it suited Gariella: a small cabin to sleep in and to shelter from storms. What caused these terrible weathers she had no idea. Someone or something. When you are a wild child, you know a lot and you know a little.

"It's me!" said Wind.

"Go back to sleep!" said she.

Wind told a lot of stories. So many that she didn't always listen. She was in the middle of her own story after all. "And cool me down when I'm hot!" she added. "If you want to be friends, that is."

"Okay!" said Wind. "Is this what you mean?" A little breeze snuffled about her as she looked over the land. She said nothing. You can ignore breezes. They are always well-behaved. But they will speak, you simply cannot stop them. Despite herself, she heard what it said.

"Someone is coming! Someone is coming! Four legs. Two heads. Very handsome! O me! O my!"

Breeze talk! Nonetheless, Gariella looked into the far, far distance.

Nothing. Nothing. Nothing.

"I will lead the visitor here," said Breeze.

"Wait! Maybe I don't want who is coming to come."

Too late. Breeze was gone. The left-behind, big yellow sun looked on as it always did, as it always did.

Maybe she couldn't control the wind as well as she thought. Gariella went over the lessons she had learned in Wind School as she called it. One brought a smile: the wind is like a cat: nearly impossible in other words. It'll stick up its tail and then jump over the fence. Here. Gone. Couldn't care less. Blink and it has jumped onto the moon. Wind tells you what to do. You don't tell it.

"Hah!" Sound of Breeze.

That was quick. Breeze was right, as right as a breeze could be: four-legged and two-headed: a most handsome frog with two squiggly legs that didn't count for much, riding a horse that clip-clopped and shook its braided mane as if to say, "I'm only doing this for the oats."

"You have come, the one I have been looking for!" spoke Handsome Frog.

"I think we have a problem here," rolled out of Gariella's mouth, always a truthful girl is she. Her blonde hair became more blonde as if in fright, as if in horror, as if maybe this is the way to disappear: fade away, fade away! It whirled about. "Let's get out of here!" it whispered. Or was that the breeze?

"Not at all a problem!" croaked Handsome Frog. "All according to the book that I read last night under the full, bright moon. Listen up, ugly and messy though you are, like a throw-it-away doll, and you'll soon be free from the wavy stuff on your head. And, well, if I were less polite, I would say 'Phew!' about that face. Sorry, I couldn't help myself. Call it getting to know each other! Please, could we have just one Croak! if only for the sake of the horse who is not used to the noises you make? I also will feel more friendly towards you."

Said horse was, indeed, bulging its eyes at Gariella, and its gaze ballooned further when she gave a "Croak!" Why not! Go along to get along, or frog along to ... oh, never mind!

"That's my princess frog-to-be!" said Handsome Frog. "Now, it says here." He extracted a book from his saddlebag, and he read, "'... And then the handsome frog closed his most-attractive-of-all, soap-bubble eyes and held his marsh breath, so liquorice-sweet, and he kissed the girl despite how she looked terrible hairy yellow, quite a fright. He was a frog for the storybooks, you see.

"'O, thank you my warts-and-all prince!' the unacceptable girl said. When Handsome Frog opened his I-really-don't-want-to-look-at-her eyes, he saw that the magic of his warty lips had worked. Beautiful, bumpy and green, with ballooning eyes, as only a princess frog can be, she had become. That's the power of a handsome frog's kiss! 'It's me and you!" she croaked and hopped behind the handsome frog onto his happy-to-have-you-both-on-my-back-if-only-I-can-get-some-oats horse. Off they rode to a mud-and-reed place where they enjoyed each other's company forever after, etcetera, etcetera,' and what could be better?

"Let's get it over with and have that magic kiss!" Handsome Frog said. "You can have your own lily pad and a share of the juiciest flies, wings plucked or not as you please. What's not to like?"

Handsome Frog hopped to the ground, closed his moon eyes before they burst, puckered the already-described lips. "I have also been called 'Irresistible'!" he said. "You may repeat that day and night."

"Irresistible! You are Irresistible!"

"Ah, yes!" said Handsome Frog. "So much better with the eyes closed! This kiss will make a lot of baby frogs in the end."

His this-is-a-moment-to-remember pucker met big squishy lips around a mouth full of teeth like a picket fence.

"Neigh!" Gariella said. "Open your all-seeing eyes, Frog Prince!"

"Neigh?"

"Neigh! Neigh! Neigh! Neigh!" Gariella pointed to a pool of water mirror. "You should be careful whom or what you kiss when you kiss," she said.

"Oh I don't mind," replied the frog that once was. He neighed at his reflection. He neighed at his what-do-I-have-to-do-next-for-oats horse. "You may call me the Handsome Horse, you may!"

"See you in another story!" said Gariella as the two horses galloped away to share the grass together and rub necks because that's what horses that like each other do.

She climbed back into the boat when a big wave showed up. It carried her away on its back. "Or are you a whale?" she asked.

"I am what I am!" Wave roared and flipped its tail.

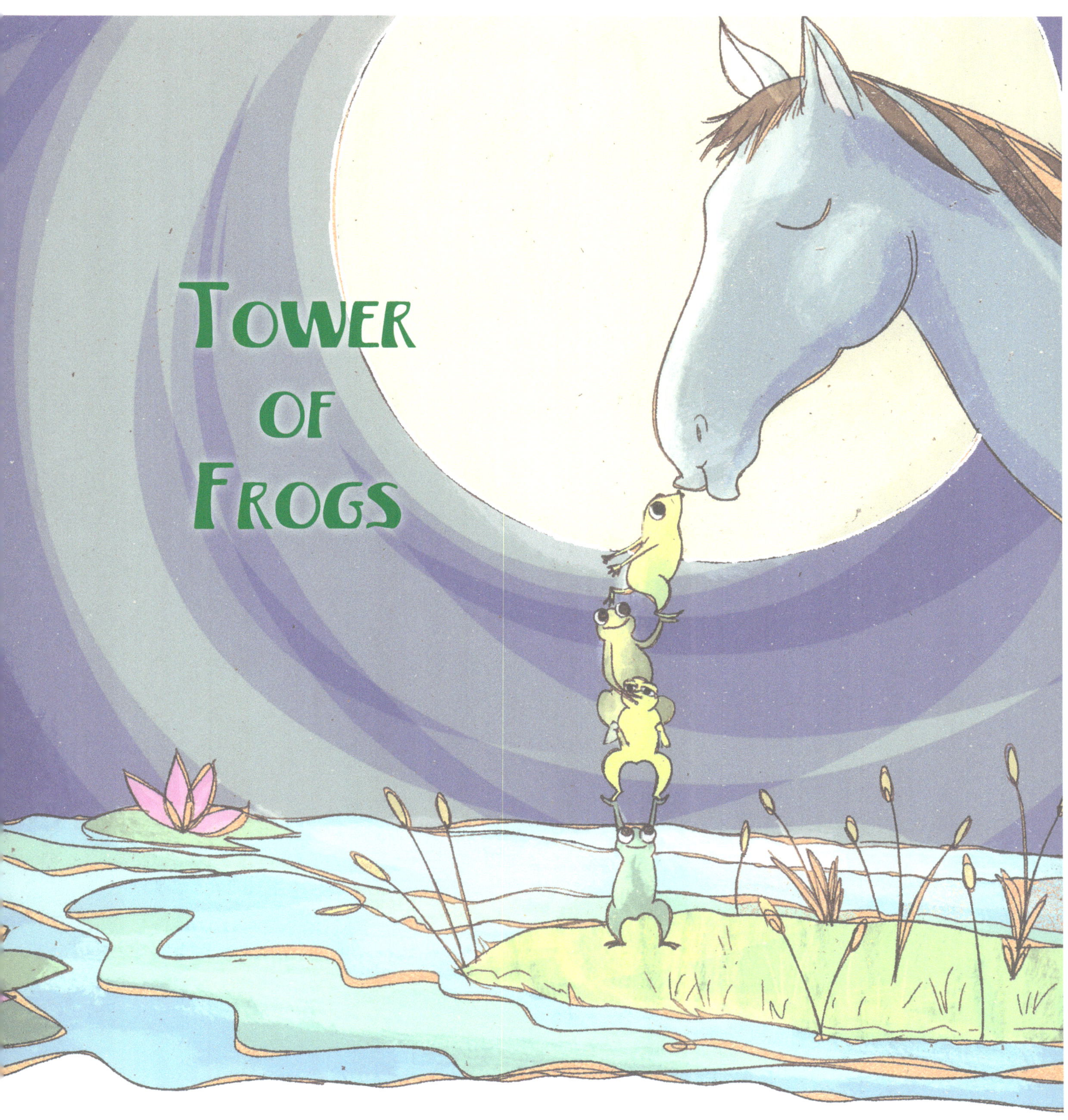

Tower
of
Frogs

Two horses in the marshland. "Why are we here?" neighed one.

"O, I have some friends to visit," the other horse neighed back.

Very annoying! The first horse tossed its braided-mane. "Who has friends in a water-logged marsh! We're up to the fetlocks in mud!"

The second horse began to croak: "Croak! Croak! Croak!"

"You are not a frog, you know, you are a horse. Your frog days are behind you. Let us go! It's muddy and wet in here. We are not the right shape or the right size as you once were."

"Croak!" said the croaking horse.

"I wonder if it's possible to take back that kiss," said the annoyed horse, "and then you can be the frog prince and ride around on my back again." First chance I get, I'll throw you off, he didn't say, into the marsh that you like so much. Now that I've tried it, I prefer not to have something on my back. Who needs a rider! Come to think of it, the best way to be free is to leave with a gallop. Some friendships should come to an end especially when started by a trick. Now there's a thought to act on, he decided, and off he galloped to a safe distance after trudging out of the mud.

"Hark!" croaked the marsh frogs.

(Hark is an old English word that is often used at Christmas when people sing a certain song about singing angels. How the frogs came to use it is a mystery although it is one of their favourite words and a special team of scientists expects to know why within the next ten years should the two frogs they are studying in church-shaped test tubes give the answer.)

"Hark! we hear the croak of the Frog Prince whom we thought had croaked while searching for someone not a frog to kiss him. Better tell Froddy to hop off the biggest lily pad afore" (an old English word suitable for when something not to like is about to happen), "afore, we say, Claudius the Fabulous, or Fab Claude the Pond and Lily Prince, discovers we didn't give him much of a chance to return once not seen under a full moon. Lordy! Lordy! We think he's back!" They alarm-croaked, alarm-croaked, alarm-croaked sufficient to wake up the baby frogs.

"O, stick their heads underwater, underwater! Hop about! Hop about! Let the Pond and Lily Prince see how excited we are to see him and back in charge of everything we do! Orders, orders, that's what we like to hear."

The first to hop was Froddy, no longer in command of all he could see. Not a lot in any event. "I'm off the biggest lily pad! I'm off the biggest lily pad!" shrunk-eyed Froddy croaked. "I've left the crown of snails behind! It won't go anywhere fast." Froddy's eyes bulged again at the waterline and Froddy's mouth gurgled what he said. "Keep the secret even if you burst! Let's prepare a feast of muddy-footed flies for the tongue of our master and ruler and biggest among us! Watch out for him! That's what I say."

Here came platters of flies ready to walk into any frog mouth because it looks interesting in there: "This is how you clean your feet, clean your feet! Maybe this is the way to China."

"He's even bigger than he was!" croaked one scum-eyed frog who had been drinking the marsh water not in the right place, not in the right place.

"He's changed shape too!" croaked another from underneath a lily pad.

"No one's been on my super-sized lily pad then?" croaked Claudius the Fab as he once was known when in another form.

"No! No! O Great Changed One!"

"Only Froddy!" croakled a baby frog, raising its head out of the water, because baby frogs can't tell a lie unless it's about themselves. They love to tell the truth about other frogs. "He sat on Lily Pad and told us what to do. It was okay!"

"It was okay? No! No! No! And not at all okay!" croaked Claudius in the shape of a horse and entirely bigger than he had been. "Bring him to me!"

Froddy's paddle to get away was a paddle too slow. He was caught and brought, and raised higher and higher from frog to frog on top of frog. "This is not so bad!" Froddy croaked. "I like it up here! I really do!" It took the right number of frogs in Marsh Land standing upon one another's shoulders to raise the excited one up to Claudius the Fab's waiting horse lips.

"Whenever you are ready!" croaked Froddy, and closed his eyes. It was their first kiss. Never to be forgotten. The moon made sure and rolled in the sky! The first kiss of all the kisses that come afterwards always feels like a frog and a horse kissing with their eyes closed. Other than that description, the experience is indescribable or, at least, completely different in another story.

"Ah, well done!" croaked Claudius, once again the Frog Prince. "There's nothing like a kiss that works backwards! We'll have to do that again, maybe in five minutes!" He hopped onto Biggest Lily Pad. "You too!" he CROAKED. "Your kiss is magic. I'm sure any horse would agree. There is room here for both of us: Claude the Fab and Froddy the Smooch! Tongue-walking flies for everyone!"

"Okay!" croaked the whole of the marsh frogs always ready to obey and to eat a fly. "Sounds good. Why not? Someone ask that other horse if it wants to have a kiss from the warty beautiful likes of us!"

"Neigh!" sounded over the marsh. "Neigh!"

"O, look!" said Baby Frog. "Here comes a big wave!!"

Sad Island
RIDICULOUS POPCORN TREE

"They all swam happily ever after, as happily as frogs can swim," squawked-squawked the seagull who had been flying above it all and preferred a fish for lunch to something that croaked.

"They did? Happily ever after! O good!" squawked back Gariella, who thought she spoke the local language. She had been alone for a whole two days since her last adventure with a frog and a kissing horse and other sensible subjects for a story. Boat bounced along from whale wave to whale wave. Or was it from whale to whale? Strong wind billowed the sail. Music, if that's what it was, played everywhere, it seemed. Something to listen to. Or imagine she heard in the rolling ocean.

Hey diddle diddle!
Hey diddle doh!
O oodles of ocean
Hey diddle O!

A head dribbling black curly hair appeared above a wave. Followed by rounded shoulders, it was. Very soon the whole of whomever rose from the sea or was whoever out for a stroll since he was above the water for anyone to see? Splash! Splash! Splash! Splash! brought him to the side of the boat.

"Nice trick," said Gariella, "if you're not a fish and can't swim. Full of air, are you? A blow-up balloon perhaps? Something without something inside."

"I am very light on my feet," the music-making, water-walking whoever said. "I weigh hardly anything at all."

"Why is that then?"

"You are what you eat."

"And what do you eat?"

"Just as I said: hardly anything at all. Would you like some popcorn? A few pops of corn?" Whoever he was, with dribbles of curls on top, reached into his pocket and held out his hand.

"Are they buttered?" asked Gariella.

"I'm afraid not."

"O well. O not well."

"You don't have to."

"I will." She popped the popcorn. "Better than nothing, I suppose. Time for a walk if you are to be believed." She stepped out of the boat. And sank up to her waist.

"Here, have a few more!"

Pop! Pop! Pop!

"That's better." She walked about. "But the thing is ..."

"Yes?"

"In the ocean it's easier to get about in a boat."

"True. But I don't live too far. Just over that wave."

"Let us see!" said Gariella. "Follow me, Boat!"

Off they went, all three together. Up and over the wave to where Whoever - she must learn his name - had said. Boat crunched on the beach. "Quiet, Boat!" she said.

The boat made no other sound. Stayed where it was and waited for what might come next.

"Welcome!" said a voice.

"A talking island?"

"It has its moments," said light-on-his-feet Whoever. "And it becomes very sad when someone leaves. It will be much happier now that there are two of us."

Two of us? Two of us? Whoever and I-Want-To-Be-Free, that's me, together! An unspoken I-don't-think-so filled all the space in Gariella's head. Nonetheless, she was curious and she was polite, and so she asked, "Why is Island so sad when you leave?" Correction: she was more curious than she was polite.

"All alone in the middle of the ocean, is it not? Quite obvious to anyone but you." Musician could be snarky too.

"Careful how you speak, Whoever!" (She no longer cared to know his name.) "But I see what you say. Waves slapping you on every side and nowhere to go, it can't be very pleasant."

"Exactly! And please call me, Musician! I am someone you ought to know."

"Although my water-slapped boat and I get along just fine,

Musician," she added. She was thinking of many things at once as anyone paying attention can tell.

"You are not stuck in one place, though, are you?" Musician looked very happy at having made that point even if it merely repeated what Gariella had said. One musical note doesn't have to be different from the one that it follows as he would be glad to explain.

"Poor Island! Poor, poor Island!" Gariella, who liked to get into the spirit of things, felt her heart throb, throb. Throb for poor island, not for Whoever.

"I am glad that you feel that way," said Musician. "Together we can help Island be in a much better state of mind!"

"And we will live on popcorn?"

"That's what most grows here. Wonderful, isn't it?"

"Maybe that's why no one stays," said Gariella. "They can simply walk away."

"Eat as much as you like!" said Island. "I don't mind how I feel, how I feel, as long as I can feel."

"The popcorn trees are - I reach can't that high - over there." A large turtle that no one noticed until it moved now pointed to a stand of trees. "So yourself help! If I could reach, I could move faster and eat some."

"Well, we wouldn't want to take advantage," said Gariella, who sat for a moment on the convenient turtle. "Island isn't

completely alone, after all," she added.

"Not the best of company," said Musician. "Fast-witted when compared to a rock but, otherwise, slow, so slow. Its words hardly ever manage to get out in the right order."

"I see," said Gariella, who didn't quite, see, that is.

"Yes, the popcorn trees don't help Island at all. Pop! Pop! Anyone who has popped and popped soon has gone, as good as popped, you might say." Musician had no interest in explaining turtles to his new friend forever or so he thought Gariella to be and, in case she was thinking that it was time for her too to be gone, he said, "I have begun a new song called, 'New Friend Forever!" Give it a listen, why don't you?

You can count on me to be
your new friend forever,
it's your lucky day, you see!
Or is it mine? O whatever!
I'm as happy as you can be.

"Too me!" said Turtle.

"Count me in!" sighed Island.

Her three new friends (she didn't include the popcorn trees – you don't eat your friends, not ever) Musician, Turtle and Island did their very best to show her what good times they would have together, for example, with their "Swing About" song:

Swing, swing, swing about

and see some more of the sea,
be happy like was me!
Happy He found She on a walk
over the slap, slap, slap sea.
And brought her back
for Island and Turtle both to sing,
"There's lots to be and be!"
Yes, when you swing about,
swing about, swing about
from he to she to thee to me!
That makes us: all for one
and one for us, us, us!

Very soon Gariella missed being at sea in her boat and away from this clearly-happy-to-be-with-her and can't-get-enough-of-her new, forever friends. Sailing into a typhoon, skittering wave to wave, with hair on sun-fire or stuck to her like seaweed in the rain, who could ask for more? However, the first rule of good behaviour is to be polite when you can't easily manage it.

"I would like to leave," she said. "You have been very friendly and clingy and that's been great. As great as very clingy can be. I'll be sure to visit again once I've sailed around the world. Big circles around the world are my thing, you see. Start here, maybe end back here, maybe not! No, it's not that simple. Ha ha!

Bye! See you as soon as soon comes!"

"Don't you want to be light as air? You won't find popcorn trees anywhere else, you know," said Musician.

"It is difficult to say no," agreed Gariella. "but a faraway place is calling for me. It's getting further and further away."

"I don't hear it," said Musician. "Wait! I'll go and put a seashell to my ear before it gets too far."

"Go if you must!" said Island. "I'm used to all of this coming and then going. I won't remember and I won't forget. One day, when there is nothing else to talk about, I will tell you about the blur."

"That is sad, I think!" said Gariella. She knew all about the blur but had no need to talk about it.

"I hear the faraway place!" exclaimed seashell-to-his-ear Musician. His dribbles of black curls now curled upwards like enchanted snakes and waved about. "Faraway Place has stories to tell," said the snakes. "Perhaps we will leave Musician and follow you! Musician or not, black curly snakes will follow you."

"You can come with me if you want," said Gariella to Musician. "I am really very generous, and snakes on the head make all the difference. Could you keep the new way you do your hair?"

Musician considered the invitation. "It's nice to be wanted. What do you think?" he asked his curling upwards snakes.

"Does that mean no more popcorn?" they asked.

"When you run out, it does," said Gariella.

"Let's go then!" they agreed. "It's not our thing, you see, whatever he says. Let him prove himself and sink in the sea in order to be your new friend forever. Wake us up when we arrive or whenever you have something to say, whichever comes first!" The snakes settled back into well-behaved, dribbling black curls.

"That settles it!" said Musician. "They have a mind of their own, you know. Wait while I pick some popcorn in case something happens to the boat. For emergencies, you see"

"I am to going stop - if I can - you." said Turtle, who got his words out wrong to them but right to him, and now stood in their way.

"I love you too," said Gariella, "but not you like a rock in the way can stop us." She patted Turtle's back and walked around him. "Goodbye!"

"Bye good! Be bye!" Turtle said.

"I'll be here when you come back," called Island. "When you finish your circle, I mean. One of many, you say?"

"Yes, when we circle the circle this way!" Boat scraped off the beach and obediently carried them away. Around the world we go, it hoped.

a Mermaid's Tail

"Here's another tune!"

Gariella rolled her eyes. How long had she and Musician been at sea, together, afloat in a boat? His disobedient snake curls whirled to the music. Octopus on a wave frowned.

It's good to be together
On a boat built for two
You can count on me to love you
Through and through and through
To sing in any weather
I'm here for you, just for you.

Jangle. Bangle. Swoozy. Woozy.

Do Do Too Doo To Do Do
Each word is a word for you.

Gariella lay flat on her back at the other end of the boat. "I don't think I can get up again." She was speaking to the sun. It listened very carefully but gave no answer. "She has to figure it out for herself," said one sun ray to another.

"I have that relaxing effect," Musician said.

Jangle. Bangle. Swoozy. Woozy.

As for the waves, they smacked the side of the boat. Tried to tip it over. They at least were on her side. Maybe she will go for a swim. Straight down will do. "Going for a swim!" Gariella said. She stood up and in she dived.

Although the water was green and black and blue and deep, all that popcorn still in her system kept her near the surface. She swam harder and harder to go further and further down. It was worth it. "It's worth it!" she bubbled. "I get all the oxygen I need from the popcorn in my belly! All is good, I knew it was right not to chew my food! Ha! Anything to get away."

Twang! Twang! Twang!

"Deeper! I must go deeper!" She passed fish with disturbed looks in their eyes. "How do we escape the music? How do we escape?" The fish bounced into each other.

A crab said, "Crabble! Crabble!" Cute. It was a cute crab.

"What are you doing?" she said. "Take my advice and get back to your reef!"

"It's crazy down there," Crab said. "I'm going to the tunes, to the tunes!"

"Good luck with that, then! Crabble! Crabble!"

When in Ocean, do as Ocean does!

Down. Down. Down. Crabble! Crabble! Bubble. Bubble.

"Look at that! An entire city! Wavy parks and twisty streets. Stacks of tiny caves and knobbly houses. Big fat policemen showing lots of teeth. Everyone dressed up: striped capes, polka dot hats, black gowns, going to the fair, the opera, the ball game, out for a soda, in for a bubble bath. Oh, look, there's something else I haven't seen before around the corner! I could write a book! Or be an under the ocean reporter! I'm sure I fit in somewhere."

"Who are you?" asked a spear-toothed shark, looking her up and down, side to side, swimming round and round. "Answer quick, quick, quick!"

Other fish gathered about. "Quick! Quick! Quick!" Flick. Flick. Flick. They butted her with their heads. They flicked her with their tails.

"I'm a visitor from Above World," she said.

"I see, I see!"

"That explains it."

"Behave yourself!"

"Watch out for the octopus!"

"O, he's on a wave."

"Was."

"Was on a wave."

"Stinging coral - watch out!"

"Ouch!"

They swam away, and so did Shark with a final "Watch yourself! I bite. I bite. Maybe another day."

Back to Musician or not? She thinks not. O look! A shipwreck! O look, a jellyfish! - "You do know that everyone can see through you. Good luck!"

"It's all my world down here. All my world down here. Jellyfish wouldn't live anywhere else for the world. Not for the world. Not for the world. Is there a world apart from me?" So said Jellyfish.

What would she do with the few bubbles of air she had left? Decisions. Decisions. O, look! What is that? Outside that cave. A sign!

BE A MERMAID
GET BACK YOUR GLOW!
YOU DON'T HAVE TO BE
WHAT YOU ARE.
VERY EXPENSIVE ITEMS
GUARANTEED TO WIGGLE!

BE A MERMAID
GET BACK YOUR GLOW!
YOU DON'T HAVE TO BE
WHAT YOU ARE.
VERY EXPENSIVE ITEMS
GUARANTEED TO WIGGLE!!

Octopus was rubbing its tentacles together when it saw Possible Customer approach.

"How much?" Gariella asked, "will it cost?"

"Gold coins will cover it. Any amount. I decide," said Octopus. Rub. Rub. Rub. "But I take credit. I follow you wherever you go until I am fully paid. By that I mean, satisfied."

"That seems reasonable," agreed Gariella. No bubbles to waste on a greedy Octopus. There must be lots of gold coins in sunken ships. "Be quick, please, I have no more air to spare."

"My latest design!" said Octopus choosing a silver and blue mermaid tail. "I make them myself. Tentacle-sewn. Machines rust down here, you see. Tried them. Don't work. One size fits all. It stretches to any body out there. Eat as much as you want!"

Gariella pulled on the mermaid tail. "Now I can speed about, go up for air and come back down. Maybe I shall sit on a rock and sing a song. An irresistible song (not like what Musician sings) that attracts a treasure boat. It will crash and sink and I'll pay you back."

"We don't want any trouble," said Octopus. "Angry Ones will come fishing after us, you'll see."

""You're right and it would be wrong. Give me a moment while I get some air!"

"Take this!" Octopus handed her a curved seashell cone. "Fill it with air for when you come back down. With it you can listen to all the ocean goings-on while you are sitting on the rock. We call it 'the latest buzzing of the buzz.' Just one more thing!"

"Yes?"

"Before you go."

"Yes?"

"Your mermaid tail."

"Yes?"

"Does not come off until I have my gold."

"Okay."

"Special glue. On your way now!"

Gariella swam away like any other fish in the sea.

"Poo Poo," the little fish followed her and said. "Go and find a rock to sit on, why don't you? Poo Poo."

Seashell

To be a mermaid on a rock
Is just my splash of sea
Whales and dolphins sing
All the current tunes
In the seashell at my ear!

Splash. Splash. Splash. Splash. "Water, water everywhere. It sure does make me wet!" Nothing like being out in the world and on a wave-smashed rock.

"We interrupt your fishy song to bring you the latest splash by splash news," Gariella heard Seashell say. "All the news you need to know:

"There are waves today and there will be waves tomorrow. Tomorrow's waves are not expected to be yesterday's waves. As for whales, whales from the North are travelling South, and whales from the South are travelling North. Clouds of little fish are getting in their way and are their lunch. What is happening today happened yesterday and tomorrow should be the same. Still, no one can tell the future today. As for yesterday, it seemed to know what would happen next. A comet could make a big splash. When it does, it will say, 'I told you so.' At the moment it's water, water, water everywhere and that is quite a lot. Now back to the entertainment with that old favourite, *I'll Meet You On The Beach Somewhere.*"

If it's meant to be,
me too!
and it's meant to be,
you too!
We'll be on the beach
together!
Not you over there
and not me over here.
Let's be meant to be
On the beach somewhere!

Another voice sounded in her other ear: "Not sorry to interrupt. How many gold coins have you collected today?"

Octopus! Greedy, never satisfied Octopus! Mermaid slapped the water with her silver and blue tail. Was it worth the price? Such a big treasure chest she had to fill! Octopus is always after her: one more gold coin, one more gold coin! Not enough! Not enough! She swam from horizon to horizon but there was Octopus waiting for her.

Octopus everywhere
was not the plan for me.
Not enough gold
to be found
for Mermaid to be free.

Mermaid's hair grew long. Every ship heard her song. "Sail on!" the Captains said. "She wants our gold. Be satisfied with what you've got, Mermaid on a rock! Sailors don't like to get wet, you know. One time is one time too many!" Yes, they remembered what had happened when they sailed too close to mermaids on rocks. "We must stay away, we must stay away! No matter how hard it is."

"Would this gently used seashell do for payment?" Mermaid asked Octopus. Black ink squirted "NO!" everywhere.

"You don't have to scream!," she said.

"You are right," said Octopus. "Sing me a song while I sit on this wave and frown at you."

"Whatever you find comfortable," said Gariella. "And takes your mind off your gold. I'll try to remove your frown." She sang to Octopus on his wave:

> Is anyone as sad as me?
> I won't lie, I won't lie.
> What I want from you
> ships in the distance
> is to come near
> to my rock where I cry out!
>
> Do try to think of me –
> Octopus rules the sea.
> Greedy tentacles everywhere.
> Give your gold, please,
> when you crash on the rock!

"Excuse me! Can I help? I heard your awful song. It's making me cry buckets here. What can I do?"

Mermaid turned. Musician stood there. Close by. Tears ran down his face. Or was it a wave had splashed him? He stopped crying when she stopped singing. "You're quite the sight, Ms. Fishtail, singing a song that no one wants to hear.

"Now let me put you in this cart!" Musician said after he carried her to shore. She couldn't say no. A musician with a plan is better than a musician without a plan, never mind a mermaid without gold for Octopus. "Stop flopping about, will you, like a fish out of water! Octopus can't follow you over land. I shall pull the cart along this path to the next ocean where you can have a nice swim with that tail of yours. There is sure to be a bumpy rock for you to rest on, and waves to splash you as much as you want."

"What happened to my boat?"

"I was lonely when you left and so I went ashore. It must be floating somewhere out there on the great wide sea."

"Octopus will pull it underwater," she said. "He's mean like that."

"Possibly. A little less talk!" puffed Musician who pulled and pulled the cart. He didn't make any music at all at least. Not sure where she belonged, Gariella flapped her tail about. Is he her hero? If she looks up "hero" in the dictionary, will it say, "Someone who pulls a cart" as an example? Isn't it a horse or a mule that does that? Better not say anything. He might stop pulling if she asked and then where would she be? A mermaid out of water needs a cart to go places and flop about in.

"If you are my hero, could you go faster?" The words came out before she could stop them. "Sorry!" she said. "I was thinking you were a horse. Or a mule."

Her hero said nothing. He had pulling to do. When they get to the ocean, he will throw her in. He had his own thoughts that he kept to himself. Something to anticipate.

"Water! Water! Nowhere! Do you think you could find me a drop to drink? I am a mermaid, you know, I need myself some water."

"Am I thirsty too?" Musician asked.

"Are you?"

"I am."

"Then a drop for me and a drop for you. Two drops will do. Before you go, I'll fan you with my tail. You don't want to frighten anyone with your sweat-drippy face."

Fan. Fan. Fan.

"That's good," he said. "You are useful after all. Better than useless. I am ready to go."

Useful after all! Better than useless! Ha! she thought. Ha!

"A drop of water! A drop of water! All I ask is a drop! For a thirsty mermaid that you don't see. She's somewhere over there in a cart. For me a drop too to be fair!"

"Here, sing us a song then and we'll drop you a drop! Or two songs for three. Two for three drops!" So said the people in the town of huts where he'd gone in search of a drink.

"That seems fair," Musician said. He opened his ready-to-sing mouth and sang,

I've been on many seas
very high on waves
everywhere, everywhere.
Turtles were amazed,
so many amazed turtles!
I've danced with an octopus
as she seemed to be,
or was it two or was it three
- so many arms, you know -
under skies really really blue
or was that under the sea?
But thirsty, thirsty everywhere
three drops now makes three.

It was a grey day. Any entertainment would do. The people opened their mouths with looks of this-is-the-day-we-have-this-much-fun!

"More than a drop! More than a drop, drop, drop for your song!" they insisted. "A bucketful of drops!"

"Not yet! I haven't ended the song."

"O please end it! We only have one bucket."

This was a very nice town with very nice people who knew a good song when they heard one. He will have to return once a year and make them happy again. He hopes they can wait until then. Maybe bring them some buckets.

Sloggle, sloggle, sloggle. Mermaid filled her tum with water. "I knew you could do it," she said. "I am right about these things. Now you can go much faster!"

"Yes we can!" Musician agreed. Pull. Pull. Pull. Into the ocean she will go. O, into the ocean she will go.

He pulled all day. He pulled all night. They arrived at the next ocean. "Puff! Puff! Puff!" puffed Musician.

"Put me in! Put me in!" Gariella ordered. "I am quite dried out."

"All right then." Musician tipped the cart and into the ocean she went. Splash!

"Now you can rest," she said. "Thank you. Bye! Stay dry!" I hope I don't need you again, she didn't say, and disappeared from sight.

Deep down she swam.

"This way!" burbled Porpoise.

"This way!" snaffed Swordfish.

"Follow me!" floppled Jellyfish.

"You can be our Queen!"

"You can rule over us!"

"You can tell us what to do!"

YOU CAN TELL US WHAT TO DO!
YOU CAN RULE OVER US!
YOU CAN BE OUR QUEEN

"That's what I am good at ('I command you! I command you!'). It's nice to be recognized," she said. Down, down, down she swam.

"Queen of the Ocean!" whispered the deep waters. "You will have a crown!" Down, down, down she swam.

Octopus better not show up in this ocean! "Stay by my side, Sir Swordfish!. You do have a point!"

"It is yours to command. Snaff, snaff!"

"Then lead me to my throne!"

QUEEN OF ALL THE
WOBBLE OCEAN
IN THE WOBBLE OCEAN

ah, here is a nice pink shell the size of her bottom. She wants to sit, sit, sit. Yes, it will do for a ruler's throne. Gariella, Queen of All the Wobble Ocean in the Wobble Ocean with waters that reach from here to there and up and down. None can measure them. None have ever seen such an endlessness of WATER! Mermaid Queen summons her whales:

"Swim about this way and that way and every which way and measure it all for me! Let me know what it is that I have! You will be rewarded, you will see. O, and any octopus you find, you know what to do."

"Glug!" said one. "Glug! Glug"

"I like a little ink with my meal," said another.

"I like a lot," said a third.

Off they gluggled, fierce-eyed on each side of each whale head. Measuring. Measuring. Sending out a sound wave for every measure.

Who can better be me?
Says Wobble Wobble Queen

Not a platypus!
Not a pussy catty puss!

Certainement (that's French
in any ocean)
Not an octopus!

Now as for this need to breathe: "Porpoises, bring me some air! Big bubbles will do. And make it fresh! Nothing recycled, no sea cow belches! Air from a breeze, not any old breeze, the best from the south, north, east or west, the highest up that you can leap, if you please!"

"What's wrong with fish breath! What's wrong with fish breath!"

"No muttering! Go!"

Off the porpoises porpoised.

"I am Queen of all that I see, and much much more!" Mermaid waggled her long scaly tail, quite pretty for a fish attachment. It would have to do, she supposed. It would have to do as long as she can fool some of the fish all of the time. Ha!

"Hello! Still in the ocean is she?" Musician rubbed his eyes and looked about. "I'll miss her if she doesn't come to the surface again. O, look! Porpoises! Have you seen an enchanting mermaid who likes to tell you what to do?"

"Queen of the Wobble Ocean, you mean! We bring her bubbles of air!"

"We bring her big bubbles!"

"Yes, sounds like her. She would want those."

"Nothing else will do!"

"It's a pleasure to serve her."

"Don't get in the way of her tail!"

"Slap. Slap."

"Yes, that sounds like her," said Musician again. "I could tell you a story or two as well."

"No time. No time. Would you mind? You are in the way of that breeze."

Porpoises gulped down bubbles of fresh air and, with flicks of the flippers, disappeared leaving Musician to stare at empty Ocean.

"Water, water everywhere and not a mermaid in sight! Perhaps a gull or two will do to pass the time. I need the latest news. No stories, if you don't mind! No fights over a dead fish! Tell me where she is and I'll drown myself close by!"

"Don't be ridiculous!" said Gull.

"Don't be absurd!" said Other Gull.

"It's all the same - ridiculous, absurd," objected Musician.

"There are differences but you are in no state to understand them."

"Look it up in the dictionary when Dictionary Day rolls around!"

"That gives me something to look forward to. Celebrating the definitions of words! What next? Smile at a Smile Day! Thank you!"

"Anytime."

"Look, a dead fish!"

"It's mine!"

"No, it's mine!"

There's more to these birds than meets the eye; of course, a dead fish shows up and then there's less to these hungry, quarrelsome birds. Musician, however, took their advice not to be absurd and that other ridiculous word. He wasn't going to drown himself over an sunken mermaid who preferred to be underwater instead of enjoying his musical company. Who would know better about how to live without a mermaid than seagulls! He was ready to sing another song to get over how he felt. Which he did, but no one - certainly not the two seagulls - paid any attention, and so no one heard it and no one could write it down. So the story moves along without it. "Hold on!" said Musician. "I must make a record of all the pain and all the heartache!" and he wrote in the sand:

Mermaids and their pretty tails
make my heart bop, bop, bop.
Seagulls squawk, squawk, squawk,
"Get over it! Get over it! Get over it!"
when mermaids stay underwater.

The tide came in before he finished writing his song and so it wasn't much work for it to wash his words away.

Next
Ocean Over

There is no anger like the anger of a fooled octopus as can be heard in the next ocean over: "She's gone! She hasn't paid me what she owes! To me! Mine! I need it all!"

One tentacle flailed this way. One tentacle flailed that way. All of the other tentacles - there were eight in total, so many that it might as well be nine - flailed every which way. Belly sucked in, Belly sucked out, Octopus swam here, Octopus swam there. At the blink of an eye Octopus was here, was there. Where did Mermaid hide in all these amounts of water, that Mermaid who owed everything to Octopus?

One eye poked above the waves. Nothing. A gull! Disgusting! Birds! Who needs them? Who would want to live in the air! Even the water won't stay up there and water goes everywhere - it drops right down. Other eye like the first that no seagull would want to see without a "Squawk!" poked above the waves. That makes two eyes. Nothing this side. Nothing that side. Another gull. "Squawk!" Tentacle reached up to silence it. Missed.

What a useless and noisy Above World! Better to go back down. All good things are in the deep. "Squawk! Squawk! Squawk!" Why are those birds squawkuawking?

Octopus tried again. Hah! Tentacle had one gull in its grasp. Second gull was curious. "Here! What happening here?" as anyone who can speak seagull would understand it to say while leaving much unsaid. Closer second gull flew to ask caught gull, "What happening here?"

Sloop! Octopus tentacle swung up and second gull flapped its wings but could go nowhere: "Screek! Squawk! Monster!"

"Now tell me, you two, what have you to say about what I want to know?" Octopus squeezed until all the latest news squawked out:

"There is a musician!"

"He's over there!"

"Next ocean. Over that hill."

"Not too far away!"

"His heart is broken!"

"We don't know why!"

"Same old story!"

"Girls. Girls. Girls."

"Boys. Boys. Boys."

"Who's to say?"

"Bunch of porpoises!"

"Yes, bunch of porpoises!"

"Thank you for squeezing!"

"We would have forgot what to say!"

"Glad to help!"

"You can let go now!"

"Porpoises swallowing bubbles of air!"

"Porpoises."

"Big bubbles!"

"Air!"

"We could use some!"

"Air! Screech! Squawk! Air!"

"Of course," said Octopus. "I can arrange that. It's my ocean. Everything on top of it is mine too. Who's to say 'No!' Show me the way!"

"Gladly!"

"This way!"

"So good to breathe again!"

"We never realized all this air was yours."

"Thank you!"

"Thank you for each breath we take."

"O do stop and lead on!" scrowled Octopus. "Not far, you say? I think I can make it." Up the hill and down the other side Octopus scroggled (what an octopus does when it travels on land).

"O! O! O!" All the spiders in Octopus's way on the land ran and hid when they saw what was coming and going past them. "All the stories are true! A spider more big! A spider more great! Bigger and Greater than all of us put together walks with a shadow that makes everything dark. Now we believe the stories! O yes we do!" The little spiders went into their little spider holes and took their medicine that made everything bad look like it wasn't bad. "It was a nightmare! A nightmare! More medicine! Yes, that feels good. Nothing is bad now!"

"But it happened in the day!" said one baby spider before the medicine took effect. "Nightmares in the daytime are the worst!" it said once the medicine took effect.

Musician had finished his song that no one heard and the water had washed away what he wrote in the sand. He might as well go back to where Boat would find him and sail from wave to wave, up and down hills of water. ("Yes, I can manage up and down, up and down, up and down," said his stomach. "No!" said the same stomach.) Maybe find another mermaid curved like a pretty wave to listen to his songs. He might even crash Boat on a rock if that's what it took. Why not?

If he sang very loud, possibly he wouldn't have to sail from wave to wave forever. A music-loving mermaid would hear him and would swim so fast to hear every word! To be at his side! Why else have a mermaid's tail? If not to swim to him! And if the wind was blowing the wrong way and she couldn't hear him, yes, he would gladly crash into a rock if that's where she sat.

Why was he wasting his time here? This mermaid once known as Gariella had used her tail to swim out of reach away. Yes, he must be going. One last look back: more porpoises swallowing mouthfuls of air. Must be a mermaid who can't breathe down there. Musician liked the logic of that thought. Yes, Mermaid might think what she liked of his songs but she would have to admire the way he could put two and two together and get clever kinds of four.

"Can you tell me her name?"

Porpoises leaped out of the water and their bodies twisted and wrote in the air: GARIELLA, QUEEN OF THE WOBBLE OCEAN, ETCETERA! That's all they said.

Reading from a distance, Octopus was sure those porpoises had lost what they call their porpoise minds. His mermaid tails do have that effect and why he must have his gold!

"Hello, Octopus!" said Musician.

"Don't speak to me!" Octopus didn't say. "Don't speak to me!" is what you think when you rush by and say nothing. Water! Octopus couldn't wait to get wet.

Musician wasn't a fighting musician. He wasn't a swimming musician. He was a water-walking musician. Maybe he'd have a walkabout. The other ocean and its lovely mermaids who would find him irresistible could wait. He would walk right over to that bubbly patch of water and look-see. Slosh! Slosh! Slosh! That's what happens when you have a heavy heart: you slosh!

Heart became heavier when Musician looked down and saw what he saw: fierce and angry Octopus wrapped about the seashell throne, fierce and angry eyes. "What do you want?" spurts of ink wrote in the water whenever anything approached.

That settles it then. No getting past Octopus, her octopus. It no longer wanted her gold, it now wanted to obey. He had better go. Slosh! Slosh! Slosh! Musician sloshed away.

"Octopus," said Gariella. "I need a king. What is a queen without a king? I don't know what kind. See what you can do!"

"Whatever you command!" belched Octopus who had swallowed too much air and with great reluctance unwrapped its tentacles from about the throne and went off in search of maybe-a-whale. Maybe a whale would do.

WHAT DO YOU WANT?

Singing Whales

"Calling all whales! Calling all whales!" Octopus sent the message out as he swam about. Belly in. Belly out. Tentacles everywhere. "Go far, clouds of little fish! Go near! Spread the word: a whale for a mermaid, Queen of the Wobble as she's known wants a king!"

"The whales will eat us! The whales will eat us! In fish school we were told to stay away from a big open mouth." The cloud of fish spun about and escaped a whale here, a whale there, all in their minds. It could have been true. It could have been true. Memories are true!

"Just say," Octopus said, "that the Queen of the Wobble Ocean in the Ocean would like the best whale to show up and rule the waters with her! You can do that, can't you?"

"Anything you say! Anything you say! Remember all that!

Remember it tomorrow! Not now! Do we have a chance to be king too?" said the cloud of fish to the fierce and angry eye. "We will find the whales and tell them what you said, tell them very fast, and get out of the way. They should be much more interested in what you have to say, being who you are - so many arms! so many arms! - than in eating us, what do you think, what do you think? What an angry eye! Anything else? No? We're off! No chance for us? No chance for us?"

Whirling cloud of fish whirled away not without a song (you can hear it when you are close):

When you're me
you're me
many times over
many times over
Add three to three
Hey, that's me and me
- there's a whole lot more! -
and me
many times over
with little bellies
little bellies
full of water.
O, o. O, o.

Search. Search. Search. Zip here. Zip there. "Whales! Whales! On the lookout for whales! Any whales here? Show yourselves!" Tiny fish voices don't travel far. "Why are we doing this? Octopus is far away. What Octopus doesn't know won't hurt us. Whales! Whales! Calling all whales!" Little fish can't seem to help themselves. Ask them to do something and they do it. Over and over. One idea fills their heads full.

It's not an easy trick to stay out of a whale mouth. Practise makes perfect sense for a lot of us to get away. All together now, cloud-burst apart!

That was the trick. Whale doesn't know which way to go.

Should Whale go this way? Or should Whale go that way? To get as many fish as possible in open mouth. Whale got a few of them. Most burst apart and escaped, that's the trick: like an exploding cloud! "Was that a yummy fish, Whale? Missed the rest of us. Hah! Hah! Hah! Chortle. Chitle. Chatle. Still lots of little fish friends left!

"This way, Whale! This way, Whale!" Fish Cloud swam away away. Back to where it started. Maybe a song contest will get the whales' minds off of tasty little fish. Leave them free to breeze about the ocean again. Breeze about. Breeze about. Join another cloud and become a bigger cloud. So many fish all the same as each other. Bellies full of water. Who can wait for it to happen? "Let's join up! Big cloud! Big cloud!"

Where one whale goes another will follow. Other whales followed. Clouds of little fish! Yum! Yum!

"Are we off the hook now? Are we off the hook now?" demanded the cloud of tiny fish. "We think we are. Yes, we are. We're gone!" And Fish Cloud went. No more Octopus time for them! No more past, present, future all mixed up. It's a new Now! What's happening? Away! Away! Up! Down! Away! Fish Cloud on the Away!

"You wanted someone to rule the ocean? We are your whales for that!" Each bigness bumped into a bigness and made the underwater "Boom!" That's a whale for you. It could push you around but, most of the time, it won't. It only has to show itself. Everything will get out of its way. "We shall decide who it will be with a the-best-song-wins contest. We can sing very well if called upon and not so bad when not called upon."

We are whales, we are whales
Nothing in the ocean
will eat us, eat us, eat us
because of our bigness,
bigness, bigness, and so
don't get in the way when
we swallow, swallow, swallow
or we shall swallow you whole.

"If that's what you say," said Octopus. "Now a real song!" Tentacles whirled about. "All together now, sing! And the best voice will win."

Whales like nothing better than an underwater concert when there's not a cloud of tiny fish to chase into each other's mouths but, despite appearances, they don't like to show off:

> We've been here
> we've been there
> we've been everywhere.
> We bump into islands
> Sometimes we burp
> We tip over boats
> It makes for quite a splash!

Tentacles stopped waving about, went to Octopus's waist like an angry teacher. "No, that's no good. Try again! Something fit for a Mermaid Queen!"

> When the moon hits your eye
> like a pie from the sky
> that's a whale of a time for you!

"No. No. No. Try again!"
The biggest whale pushed forward:

If you don't choose me,
it'll be octopus ink
that we will drink,
my friends and me,
whether or not
we are thirsty!

Now what do you say
to that? Let me be more clear!
I wanna win, and so I win.

If you want me to rhyme it
A tentacle here, a tentacle there
And no glue to make a pair. -

You know what I mean
If you wanna be as you are
instead of all separate like.

I could go on and on
and so let's get it over!

Tell us now that I won!

"And the winner is ... you!" Tentacles applauded. "Beautiful words and a most lovely tune. This way, please!" Octopus pointed to the prize.

Mermaid in her built-of-water palace was reading a book from the local Coral Reef Library while crabs-in-waiting combed her hair. The book told a story of sunken ships and deadly pirates with one eye seeing everything and one eye behind a black patch seeing nothing if it was there.

"Curls! I said, 'Curls'! Mermaid curls, if you please." The crabs had ideas of their own.

"We like the electric look, the electric look! It's what's in fashion when the super-charged eels are out about."

"Disobedient crabs! Here, do my fingernails, and behave yourselves!" Maybe she would change her mind about wanting a King. Why share the ocean? One ruler is better than two. Or would that musician, after all, do? For when she wanted to complain, that is. She lay the book down, and the book scuttled away. It too had a song, a mutter-mutter song:

Back to the library!
Back to the library!

You can borrow me
I'm on the shelf
You can read me
Not for too long.
I will remind you
when to pay a fine!

Mean Book, who only got paid by slow readers, went back to sleep on the coral reef shelf. Where it dreamed and muttered to the other books, "What did you earn today?" and they muttered back, "This is no way to make a living."

Yes, she thought of Musician and that could be important! He must have been up to something interesting since last seen. Oh no, look who's coming!

"Octopus! What do you want? My ocean! My sharks! Watch your tentacles! No more gold for you!"

"You sent for a King," Octopus reminded her.

"Ah yes, you are now under my command, as it should be. You found a King! Excellent. Bring him to me!"

"Out of the way! Out of the way!" Biggest Whale came forward and butted Octopus aside. "I can sing. I'm already as good as a king. better in fact. You can ride on my back! I'm the whale for you." Whale's mouth curved upwards on each side - that's a smile in any ocean - and a sweep of the tail swept away all the fan fish, fan crabs and fan eels that hung about.

Sir Swordfish said, "Good day!" And, "Come to the point!"

"Watch and wonder!" Whale said. "Let's have some space here! Let's have some space here! A song is about to happen!" Whale's song began to happen:

Big as you could possibly want I am
and so what's not to like about me ...

"Hold it! Hold it!"

"Something wrong, Mermaid Queen? I am a whale of a whale, you know. You should watch and wonder and not interrupt."

"You are not quite what I had in mind," whispered Mermaid who had become quite breathless. Whale and Queen of the Wobble Ocean stared at each other.

"What in all the ocean do you mean?" retorted Whale showing all its teeth and its big pink tongue.

Mermaid flicked her tail. "How can I put this? We are not the same." Again she whispered.

"What else is new!," argued Whale. "I can't imagine what it's like to be you."

"As long as we understand each other. Sing your song then and be on your way!"

"That's reason enough to be here! I will sing and be glad to be gone." Whale tipped upright, very dignified, squiggled its tail and began again but with a difference:

Big I am and far away I go
It's where I plan to be after here
Sometimes I come up for air
And then I sink back down.

It's an exciting life, anyone can see
Chase me here! Chase me there!
You think you can harpoon it.
Underneath the boat I swim,
and up and over it goes.
Drowned sailors everywhere!

"Would you like a few more lines? At this point I like to hum a bit. Humm! Humm!"

"Humm?" hummed Mermaid.

"Yes, humm," answered Whale. "Humm! Humm!"

"No more, please!" she said. "Or I will change my mind and make you King Hummer. And then where will you be? Not far away as you like it. You must go and tip over a boat. That is very important whale work." Yes, if she were a whale, it would be what she would do. She would very much miss tipping boats over and over. She can't hurt Whale's feelings, especially a big fella like him with lots of feelings ready to take over.

"Do I still get a prize then?" said Whale.

O dear! What can it be? Whale looks as though Whale already has everything.

"A mermaid's kiss, will that do?"

"Never tried that."

"One kiss then." She remembered the frog and the horse. Would she turn into a whale? Would Whale turn into a mermaid?

My! My! So much lip, lip, lip. It goes on and on. This kiss should last for at least a month and a day. Still, she wasn't sure if this was right. If she remembered her stories and adventures, anything, just any strange and unexpected thing can happen with a kiss. No, she wouldn't take the chance, and beckoned instead to a fish at her side - a Puffer Fish as it nicely happened with a good set of lips, or smackers as they are known in some circles. "Just give that big fella a wide smack on the lips for me, will you? You'll never get another chance like this."

She didn't have to whisper twice. "Don't mind if I do!" Every Puffer Fish's dream, after all, was to kiss a whale! A lot of books in a certain section of the Coral Reef Library say so. They can't, in fact, stop muttering about it in their dreams. ("Kiss me, whale, and I won't tell unless someone reads this book! Ha! Ha!") Puffer Fish planted the softest, sweetest Puffer kiss on those big, flabulous lips.

"Another! Another!" Whale said.

Puffer Fish, however, had fainted completely away. When it came to its senses again, "No more getting ideas from books or readers of books," it poofed. Nonetheless, it went in search of another whale away somewhere. A whale's kiss is an acquired taste, they say. "One more kiss and I will see," said Puffer Fish. "And then no more, or one more and one more and one more."

For all its get-out-of-the-way bigness, Whale was a good whale and didn't push Mermaid off the throne or toss her out of the ocean when she said, "No more! No more! One kiss was the deal."

"I shall remember forever," Whale said, "your most Puffered kiss! You will hear me sing about it all over the ocean."

Here now, not here now, and Bigness with a wobble was gone!

GOT TO
LOVE MERMAIDS

He loved a mermaid
She was so cruel
His heart is broken
He is such a fool

What made him think
She loved him true?
Was it his songs
That told him so?

What's in a song
has to be true!
It's not all made up
and then sung about,
sung about like a fool.

Maybe not! Maybe not! Musician sloshed in circles of "Maybe not!" One Ocean Over she was but he could not get Mermaid out of his mind. It didn't help that all the mermaids in this ocean disappeared as he searched for a second-best replacement. Maybe they weren't actually there. Did real mermaids exist? Was he seeing mirages? He would find a doctor and have his temperature taken. Some anti-mermaid pills should fix him up. It's a mermaid fever he had.

"Doctor! Doctor! Can you check me out?"

A passing ship took him on board, and its ship doctor applied a stethoscope and a thermometer to his nose, throat, chest, back of the knees. "Feel that? Feel that?" With a grin that said "This will hurt you more than it hurts me!", the medical person banged him on the knee with a hammer.

"I felt that!" Musician said.

"You are fine. You need a rest from mermaids, that is all. Whether real or imaginary, it only takes one of them to give you a fever. Take this Quick Fix Pill. It will make you not believe the way you are now."

"Yes, there's something wrong with the way I am now." Musician swallowed the Believe It Not Pill, as he renamed it. "From its size that should work or nothing will," he said and looked down at his swelling tum. "Already seems to be having an effect."

Nurse in a white uniform with no blood on it yet tucked him into bed. He seemed to be awake. He seemed to be asleep. Nurse must have left the round porthole window open when she went away because Ocean was coming into the cabin. He should get up and close it. Get up from the bed where salty sea water rose about him. Shark swam in. Swam through the little round porthole. Swam round and round inside the cabin. Maybe what Musician believed before he took the pill was better!

"Come with me!" Shark said. "Follow me!" It showed Its teeth and swung its tail.

"Of course. I shall rise from this sickbed and go with you." You don't say no to a shark, not if it speaks nicely and it hasn't yet eaten an arm or a leg, and you see your reflections in its shining teeth. Musician rose.

"What next?"

"Believe it or not, you're all Fixed Up! That's why you can breathe underwater. Easy-Peasy!"

He would need another pill not to believe the big fish. At least Shark seemed to know what was happening. "I'll keep believing then, shall I?" Musician said.

"That would be best. You have some experience believing things, I understand."

BELIEVE IT NOT

"Mermaid experience. Does that count?"

"O, it counts! You will believe anything if you think a mermaid is interested in anything but gold .Snoik! Snoik! Now come with me before you get any other ideas in that musical head!"

"One more question."

"Yes."

"Did the ship sink?"

"O yes, it hit Mermaid's Rock. Come! Let's go!"

Out the porthole Shark swam, Musician close behind. Did anyone else on the ship survive? Except him? It's a good thing to survive. Swim. Swim. Swim. They passed the captain of the ship who saluted as they went by. "I am the Captain!" he said. "I went down with the ship."

"Yes, so did we all," Musician said. "So did we all. I suppose you didn't see the rock, in the dark and all."

"It was daylight!" Captain said. "I was looking the other way. Won't happen again. 'Never look at a mermaid!' I was told at Ship School. 'Never look at a mermaid! It will make you crash into a rock.' I was told that one was there. Next time I'll look where the ship is going, although there may not be a next time."

"No, suppose not. Well, good luck if there is a next time! We - Shark and me - are going up there. You can just see the sky from here. Have to go."

"Yes, above the water is good," Captain said. "I'll stay below. With the ship. With the ship."

"I'M THE CAPTAIN"
"I WENT DOWN WITH THE SHIP"

On Mermaid's Rock, Musician stood. With Nurse and Doctor looking ready to go to work in their white uniforms, he stood. "You've recovered nicely, we see," they said.

"I owe it all to your Quick Fix Pill. And to Shark," he added.

Shark swam round and round Mermaid's Rock. "Did I do the right thing? Maybe I should have been thinking about myself. I'm hungry now. Come here, something to eat! A little closer please. I have such an empty tum! You owe me, you know, for payment. I will take a bit at a time. Not all. Not all. That's fair, I think."

"O, I would help if I could," Musician answered.

"Just stick a thumb in the water, would you? And I'll have a nibble. Gentle-like. You'll hardly notice a tickle."

"That's a reasonable request. Here have a whole arm!" Musician said. "Least I can do. A big fella like you must have an appetite."

"No! No! No!" Musician heard.

"What's that? The beautiful sound of 'No!' Can it be that someone cares for my arm? Not you, Shark! If they care for my arm, possibly, maybe, they also care for what is attached to it, me? It can't be Mermaid. Too bad! She's one ocean over, and so who could be saying, 'No! No! No!'?"

"Us! No! No! No!" Three Mermaids popped into view, golden tails curved above the wave. All spoke the same thing at once.

No! No! No!

"Where were you when I needed you?" Musician said. "I looked everywhere."

"We like to be secret," Three Mermaids said. "We don't want to end up in cages and zoos!"

"You all speak together, as one!"

"Yes, we do," said the three mermaids. "Go away, Shark!" Shark swam away.

"Imagine that!" it said through its teeth, through its teeth.

"How can I thank you? You have saved my arm and, I suppose, me. After all that I have been through it's difficult to know quite what is best to do. Perhaps there is a pill for that."

"You can say, 'Thank you!' No need to be medical. It's not hard at all."

"Thank you!" said Musician. "And may I ask one more thing?"

"Yes."

"That beautiful word, let me hear it once again!"

"No! No! No!"

The three mermaids arched their backs, rose up higher and dived back into the water.

"Well, what do you think of that?" said Musician.

"Talking porpoises," said Doctor.

"Rare. Very rare," said Nurse.

"But not unknown," said Doctor.

"You didn't see mermaids?"

"No. No. No." Said Doctor. Said Nurse. Together. "Time for another pill, another pill. Join us, why don't you?"

"I think not," said Musician. "I believe mermaids are the cure for me!"

OCEANS
APART
YOU HAVE
BEEN SUMMONED!

usician and Mermaid. Forever and Forever. Was togetherness meant to be? Wet cuddles and wet kisses. Holding hands in the sea. Not meant to be if separate oceans had anything to do with it. He's here. She's there. Did she still not care to share an ocean?

"This is a lot of water I've got here," said Musician, "and I am free to do as I wish. Sing loud or not. Maybe it's better this way. Hey Parrot! Don't land here! Do what you want to do! Not what you have to do for a cracker. You're free as a bird: if you stay up there, that is."

Something white landed on Musician's head.

"Silly bird," said Musician. "Where did you come from? Can't help its natural functions. Hey!" A lot of white rained down and splattered him. "You are definitely eating too much, and this effect of it is not welcome." Musician jumped from Gariella's boat that had floated by one day, and washed himself in the sea.

Next ocean over, "It's completely ridiculous," said Mermaid to herself. "I don't like Musician at all. And yet he is in my mind like a song on the radio. I change the station and he keeps singing. He is singing some made-up song again! He'll take any excuse to open that singer of his. Why, he would sing about a pebble in a shoe!"

Which talk of songs rattling in the head reminds her that she hasn't seen her feet lately. They haven't felt a pebble in a shoe for the longest time. She hasn't painted her toes that are always so pleasing to look at. When is the last time she wiggle-waggled them? Not much she can do in a fish tail. Swim here. Swim there. She would rather go for a walk and have the sand between her toes than suffocate in a fish tail! Where is Octopus? Didn't Octopus say, a few stories ago, that only he could unstick the special mermaid tail glue?

"Octopus! Octopus! Get your many tentacles over here! I have something for you to do. Immediately!" She had to act the part of being in charge if she wanted anyone to obey her. "Go, Lobster, to Octopus with my command!"

"You have been summoned! You have been summoned! Our Terrible Queen, that is, our Mermaid Queen calls. You know, Ms. Fishtail over there!" While Lobster spoke, it whack, whack, whacked its little head with its big lobster claw to make sure it got everything out with the result that Octopus heard nothing it said.

Octopus looked up from all the books Octopus was writing at once - so many stories in the ocean, and the library ever muttering, "One more, one more, here's space for one more!"

"What is it, Crack-A-Brain?"

"The Queen! The Queen!" Lobster burbled.

"I know her," Octopus said. "Always has her tail in a twist! What's she want now?"

"You! You! Now I must go. I have a dinner appointment. I am to be picked up in a very nice travelling compartment, they're expecting me!"

"Poor Lobster! You'll never learn, will you? But you will look very tasty on a dinner plate next to a pile of string beans. So very, very hot pink you will be against the green!"

"Thank you. Most kind! Most kind! Care to join me?"

"Later perhaps. It all depends. I am a specialty item, you see, and I don't go without a fight" Octopus put away his writing materials and had a think, as anyone could tell because his tentacles wrapped about his head when he thought, or whatever it is that a brain full of ink does.

YOU HAVE BEEN SUMMONED!

Yes, when an octopus thinks, a lot of ink swirls around in its big brain which is why, according to some really deep-thinking storytellers, think and ink are nearly the same word. There are less thoughtful people who have a completely different opinion on the matter, or no opinion at all, but never mind about them.

Octopus had dark thoughts - thoughts the colour of ink, in fact, as they must necessarily be with a creature such as he. To obey! Or not to obey! That is the question Octopus must decide. He bulged out. He bulged in. Finally, "I'll see what Mermaid Queen wants and then I'll decide," Octopus decided. "Always ordering me about! If it's not this, it's that. If it's not that, it's this." Octopus bulged in, bulged out. Sometimes, to be the main course at a fine restaurant and get some respect doesn't seem such a bad idea. At the last moment, his tentacles would reach out and tighten around everyone's neck, hok! hok! - That's something to put in a story after he had ended everyone else's story. Hok! Hok!

I don't think,
I think up
stuff to do.
To anyone thinking
Of cooking me,
it's called
Imagination.

Tentacles waving, Octopus arrived. "What's up then? I am yours to order about. Once more. And that's one last more or the last once more." O no! Had he gotten ahead of himself and already decided to obey without having heard the command? You have to think quick to be ahead of yourself, he said, he said, and made himself feel better.

"What's wrong, Octopus? Not happy, are we?

"Happy as happy can be serving the Queen of the Sea. Must be why I have all of these arms. What better to do with them? Write a book, massage a whale, you scratch my back and I scratch all your friends' backs ... lots to do."

"Octopus, I would like to go for a walk but, as you see, it's quite impossible with this thing ..." Mermaid flapped her mermaid tail.

"Yes, I see. I'm not a fan either. Wouldn't be caught dead in one. Or two or three in my case. An octopus mermaid! A meroctopus! Hok! Hok!" Octopus laughed. "Yes, I am happy as happy can be. Let me see what I can do!"

Many tentacles took ahold of the blue and silver tail and pulled and pulled.

"Won't work. You said it was glued."

"I did, but it isn't. Glued, that is. A tight fit, that's all. Didn't want you thinking you could escape, did I? It's the usual lesson: don't believe everything you're told. Hok! Hok!" Octopus bulged in. Octopus bulged out. "Heave-ho! Heave-ho! Heave-ho!" Thwop! Away came Mermaid's tail.

"O look at my pretty toes!"

"Yes, lovely I'm sure. Where did you acquire them? I must get some myself. Cheaper by the dozen, are they? Some have six per foot, you don't say! Eight legs here. Hok! Hok! Now, if that's all, I have a place to be, to be. Or not to be. Your toes are confusing me. Do they grow very, very long? Maybe when they do, I might like you a bit better. We could message each other so much. I said message, not massage."

"Silly Octopus!" Gariella, shuddered to think what might happen if her toes did grow. In order to get away from these unacceptable ideas she went for a bottom-of-the-ocean walk. "O, one last thing, Octopus," she said over her shoulder, "Bring me Musician!"

"Luckily I have a big brain," Octopus said, "And it knows how to do big things!." Octopus flew, it was a sight to see: Octopus, like an underwater helicopter, whirred to the surface of the ocean. Tentacles whirred and whirred. Octopus should have tried this a long time ago. That's what happens when a mermaid commands, even a pretend mermaid: everything obeys with a whirr, whirr, whirr. Helicopterus, call it what you will, whirred and whirred until LIFT-OFF!

"I'm up! I'm away! To the next ocean I go!"

Helicopterus flew over the land that divided Ocean from Ocean. All the tiny spiders below scurried away. "He's back! He's back! The monster can fly!"

"Yes, there is the other Ocean. Lots of waves, lots of water. Must be it. Time to descend." Whirr. Whirr. "Let's have a look-see! Musician, Musician, where can Musician be?" Splat! "Whoops. Should have put on the anti-whirr. Do I remember how to swim? Yes I do. Musician is not on the water. Maybe he is below."

Swallow enough ocean and become good and sick of Mermaid, so Musician had decided. If too much of a good thing is bad for you, then too much of a bad thing - seawater inside you - should work even better at being bad, and seawater reminded Musician of Mermaid, which made a bad thing a good thing in a way and easier to do. He opened his mouth. Sea in. Sea in. Sea In. Yes, that's it. Quite full. He floated, floated, floated under the water. Fish, fish, fish bumped into him. "What's this? What's this? Something new has floated into the neighbourhood!

"Let's go! It could bite from some secret place. It looks like one of those air monsters above the water. It won't fool us! Spit! Spit! Let it know how we feel! Ptui! Hey!"

With his tentacles Octopus swept away all the onlookers at an accident and dragged Musician back to Mermaid Rock. Laid him flat. Tentacles pushed the front of him. Tentacles pushed the back of him. Push. Push. Pushed the front of him until a bucket's worth of sea spurted out of Musician's mouth. "Gasp! Spew! Gag! Thank you for the massage!

"I'm alive! I'm alive! I was not meant to die!"

"If you say so," said Octopus.

"This return to air must mean I am going to be happy and all my wishes will come true once I make some new wishes. I could sing a song!"

"Please!" Octopus said. "Later perhaps. Not now. Think of your lungs, what they've been through!" Think of me, Octopus didn't say, out of extreme kindness for the patient.

Mermaid! Mermaid!
Has sent Octopus
For me! For me!
It's meant to be!

"Yes," said back-to-life Musician of his latest composition, "that's a good beginning and the rest should write itself as the rest happens. Mermaid must be impatient to see me. Let us go, Octopus! Which way? Which way?"

"That's right. Leave the rest of the song till later!" said Octopus. "Now, a lot larger I will make myself - a bulge I can do for a passenger or two - and straight up! After we get a start in the water first. Climb up top! Hold on!" Splash! "Now back up we go!" Whirr! Whirr! Whirr! "That's my tentacles you hear."

MERMAID ROCK

"Such a nice sound! Can I borrow it for a future song?"

"Be my guest!"

Octopus - Helicopterus - made the delivery. "I'll just drop you here. She's down there somewhere. It's all up to you. Up to you. My job's done." Splash-splosh! Sound of a musician dropped into water with arms and legs whirring about.

Musician held his breath. Musician whirred down helicopterus-style. And there was Mermaid, girl-of-his-song! Easy-peasy. He had no breath to make a big search. There was Mermaid! Standing on her own two feet. No more fish tail! That means no more Mermaid.

"What do you have to say for yourself?" Gariella asked. "I shall give you one more chance to amuse me. I am good that way."

Did he have enough breath left to speak? "Will you GURGLE! GURGLE! with me?" Musician said. "Those are pretty toes," his air bubbles managed to add.

Gariella rolled her eyes. What was it with everyone and the toes! "You do need help. Yes, I'll gurgle, gurgle with you. Now keep those lips closed. The water goes in, you know. Keep that smile, if you like! Think of a song - anything to keep you alive and move our story along!

"Octopus! Octopus!" she called.

"What now?" Octopus's tentacles pointed here, pointed

there. Octopus would rather be anywhere but here. "I knew I should have gone back to the other ocean. One last time, that's all, and then you'll have to finish the story yourself! I am as big as I can get, so hang on tight!"

"Thank you, Octopus. Please, take us back to the boat and you're done!"

"Promise?"

"Cross my toes if that's your thing."

Whirr. Whirr. Whirr.

Musician sang:

Whirr-whirr-whirr

whorr-whorr-whorr

Look at the lookedy land below

it's skylilly nice up here

cloudy and bluey

and wind-windy too –

that's why my arms

are happy about you.

Gariella sang back:

Yes, it gives you the chance

to take a chance with me.

Once we are back down below
we shall soon see
who is in charge
and it won't be you.
Tighter if you would,
it's wind-windy up here.
And don't drop me
Or it won't be good for you.

"A few more rehearsals and we'll tour the ocean together,"
Musician said.

"Not on me!" Octopus whorred.

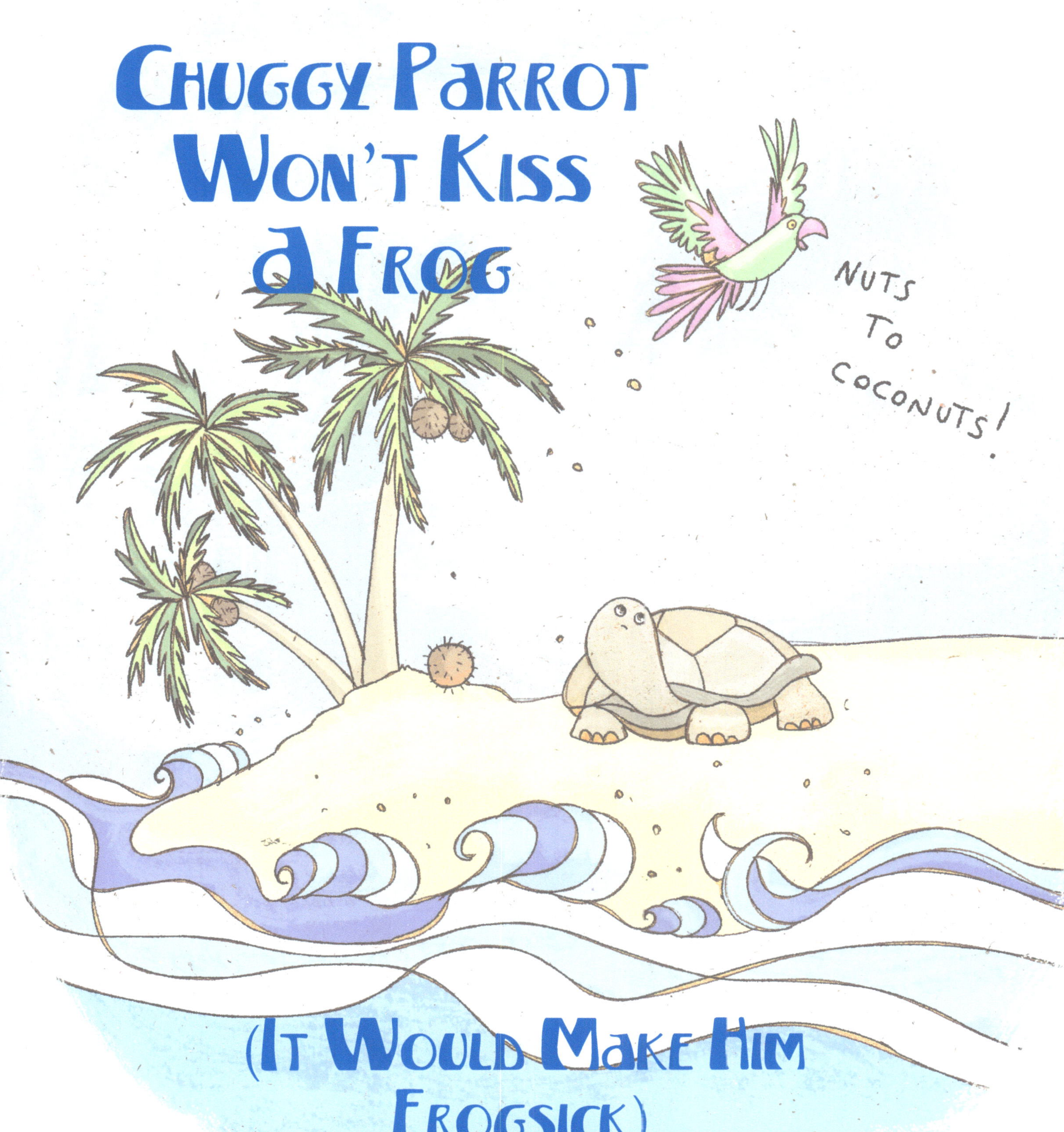

Chuggy Parrot
Won't Kiss
a Frog

Nuts
To
Coconuts!

(It Would Make Him
Frogsick)

"**W**ell, that was a whirr!" Gariella had her feet up in the back of the boat. Billowing wind billowed the sail like a well-fed whale belly.

Next to her, Musician held the rudder. "I have another whirr-whirr song in mind!" He said.

"Later! Much later!" she requested.

Musician agreed. "Shall we go back to the island and say hello?"

"Island. Island. All alone. Yes. Sad Island will be happy to see us. Steer to it, Musician, and maybe when we get there you can sing it a song. Meanwhile asleep is what I need to be. Please do not disturb!"

"Who me? Disturb? Not I! No. No. No. No."

"And do not 'no' any more after that last no!"

With lips closed Musician steered from wave to wave. Slap. Slap. Slap. "Hush waves! Hush now!" he would have liked to be able to say. From quiet wave to quiet wave he steered.

"Snoggle, snoogle. Snoggle, snoogle."

Goodness! What is that? Who maketh these pretty ugly - or ugly pretty (not the same thing) - sounds? Snoggle? Snoogle? Overboard with whatever is making that disturbing-to-Gariella noise! She has a pile of sleep to work through and she likes to take her time.

Musician turned to find wherefrom the snoggles came. He looked. Looked. Looked again. Never would have thought it! Never! He had such ideas about the girl, an otherwise perfectly song-worthy, girl in a boat. When awake and in his arms travelling by octopus in the sky, as he would never forget, her breath flutters like a dreamed up breeze. But now! snores and sniggles tumbled from little Ms. Full-of-Complaint's open mouth. Tumbled across the deck and flopped down with a snoggling last breath. What a mess! Snoggles everywhere! He couldn't get them out of his musician's ears.

"Blow, Wind! Blow! Do something about these snoggles hurbling and curbling from Ms. Not-At-All-Melodicious!"

Wind didn't want to get too close to the racket, but Wind was in charge of the neighbourhood and so it tidied up, it swept and blew. It blew lots of air into Gariella and, after a terrible battle, the snoggles stopped.

"Thank you, Wind!" Musician said. He steered Boat from wind-shaped wave to wind-shaped wave. Up a mountain of water, Boat climbed. Down a mountain, Boat slid. Island, Island, O so far! Maybe Island can meet them halfway. After stuffing a dream into Gariella's head to keep the snoggles away, Wind carried Musician's thought on its journey, blowing birds out of the way and riding the waves that it formed as it went.

Whatever Gariella;s dream, a big grin had replaced the snoggling mouth. Maybe all girls are like this: difficult and easy depending how the wind blows, each girl a different pretty lump. So thought Musician as he whisper-sang to himself:

What a pretty lump is she

no matter what she does to me,

For her I'd be a pirate

and teach a singing parrot

like one I saw yesterday

- I'll rhyme that with a carrot! -

to sing a song to her, to her.

That should become very popular with a bit of work. He could hear it now sung simply everywhere. "What A Pretty Lump Is She." Good title. Good beginning. As for the rest, pirates and parrots fit each other very well. And a musician would fight like a pirate for a carrot if he had to, if he had to. If she asked him, on very hungry days. Yes, stick that in somewhere! And a parrot maybe would sing a song for a carrot. That, according to Musician, is how to throw a song together.

"Island is straight ahead," Wind said. "I must get there with Musician's request that it meet them halfway. Nothing could be more important. Blow! Blow!"

"Chug! Chug!"

"Chug chug out of the way, Parrot Bird! No flying thing stops Wind. The sky is mine! BLOW!"

"Chuggy will fly over the top of Wind. Chuggy will fly to the side. One way or another Chuggy will go wherever Chuggy wants. Go! Go! Chug this way. Chug that way.

"By the way, Wind, Chuggy loves its Chuggy name. You thought it would be Polly, but it's not. It will soon be the name of choice in all the parrot stories. By far. By far. Chuggy the Parrot! Now on your way to the important place while I sing an important song that introduces me."

A chuggy parrot
flew over the sea
Sailors on their ships
taught it to sing

any which way
they might want
That's how to get
a cracker with butter
and jam and tea!
Chug, chug, chug.
No one sings a song
or chugs tea like me!

Where does Parrot come from? Where does Parrot go? It's not easy-peasy when there's no land to see. Flap flap, flap flap is how a parrot flies from ship to ship and to any other place where it's solid to land on. More self-introduction:

Parrot on an island
not long ago
- it was the other day -

As for tomorrow
it won't come.
It's always today
on an island
in the sea.

No one to listen to
no one to copy
except for coconuts
when they fall
from the tree: "Boom!"

"Boom!" Parrot says,
"Boom! Maybe
far, far away
is more interesting;
Nuts to coconuts.
Bye-bye! Bye-bye!
Popcorn makes me
fly too high."

Island enjoyed Parrot's company while it lasted. All good things come to an end. Not best things. Best things come back. That's what Island believed and no one had ever said, "No!" Island looked up at the best sun. Today. Tomorrow. Forever. And that's the best cloud. That's the best rain. That parrot will be a best parrot when it comes back. So Island believed. And what Island believed usually came true. There wasn't much that could go wrong, you see.

NUTS
TO
COCONUTS!

"Hello, Wind!" Best wind is back. O, Island knew what it knew. Island knew what it knew. Blow hard! Blow soft! Yes, Wind, Island does what you tell it to do. Birds flutter whipsy doopsy, hide in the sway sway, bend bend trees. Island and Wind know each other a long time. Wind visits but does not stay. Sometimes Island gets too much in the way and both of them feel sick the next day.

Listen to the wind, Island! It has something to say: "You have visitors coming, they want you to meet them halfway. Fat chance! Fat chance! Wind knows it is not possible but Wind said that it would say."

"I'll give it a go," Island said. And pulled at everything of itself underwater. "No, I am here to stay."

"A push at the back," Wind said. "Always glad to help." And Wind whirled around. "No. No. Puff. Puff. No good. I'm off! Find me over there." Wind wandered away.

"Best clean up the place!" Island said. "Can't look like this when visitors arrive. Can't look like this when they arrive. Wind always leaves a mess. Whichever way Wind blows, Wind leaves a mess."

"Ok!" Turtle said. "I'll over start there."

"Don't bother!" Island said. "It'll all come together by itself and they will be here before you begin. Maybe you can meet them. When in the sea, you are an island after all and a speedy one at that."

"I'll catch the next wave out," Turtle said.

Flapping from wave to wave, Parrot lands on Boat.

Island is close!
Island is close!
Close. Close.
Close. Close.
How else
could I get here?

Parrot perched on the prow of the boat. "This is my boat!" as good as spoke its speaking eye. One side of Parrot's head faced the sea, the other side faced the boat. "I am willing to share if you let me perch here," its eye also said. And, "A cracker will do, if you have it. Forget the butter. Don't forget the tea! I'm easy to please. Once you get to know me, you will give me more." Parrot had a very speaking eye.

Gariella and Musician didn't need to be told what a parrot wants. It's in all the stories, after all. And that's why it's necessary to read, read, read. So that you know what to do when a parrot shows up and takes over everything and is right away in command.

THIS IS MY BOAT!

"Here, in the bottom of the boat, should be popcorn." Musician proffered what he found in the palm of his hand. One parrot eye looked, other parrot eye looked. All right, Chuggy obliged, as a favour, and pecked at one or two popcorns. Without a flap of the wings Parrot rose into the air. "Good stuff!" Chuggy said. "It's why I had to leave Island. Too high! Too high! You, though, could walk on the sea if you eat enough of that."

"Yes, it has that effect." Gariella said. "Is Island close? Is Island close? Did you fly from it? Did you fly from it?'

"That's right, say it twice," Musician agreed. "That's how to speak to a parrot. You are so knowledgeable, I could sing a song to your lots of knowledge." But Parrot sang instead:

Island. Island. Island

Close. Close. Close

Higher, higher

I go, I go

It's closer, closer.

Popcorn. Popcorn. Popcorn.

More. Less. More. Less.

Island wasn't close, but Parrot thought so. It felt so. "O Parrot!" Gariella said. "O Parrot! We sail and sail and sail. And Island is further away and further than far away, it seems and that's much the same as it is."

Further than far?

Further than far?

Island is near.

Island is near.

It seems not.

It seems not.

Chuggy's boat.

Chuggy's boat.

Is here. Is here.

It seems. It seems.

Chuggy walked along the railing of the boat. Sang to the waves, Sang to the sky. Stared at two sides of the world - right and left - at once. Sang to himself: "Chuggy sings!" Parrot flew up into two worlds at once. And flew back down. "'My boat! My boat!' Chuggy sings!"

"No more popcorn," Gariella said. "No more popcorn for that bird."

"No high Chuggy! No high Chuggy! No high Chuggy!"

"That parrot needs help," Musician said. "Maybe Wind will come back and sort him out." He remembered its success with Gariella's snoggles.

Night came instead. Stars blinked awake. "You're looking good," one star said to another. "Nice spangle dress. Where are you going tonight?"

"O, same place, always a good time to be had there."

"Anything happening below?"

"Earth, you mean?"

"Yes, that round ball down there."

"Let's spin it around and see!"

Spin. Spin. Spin.

"Looking up makes you dizzy," Gariella and Musician said. They lay in the bottom of the boat with the night sky blinking its many eyes at them.

"Dizzy! Dizzy! Dizzy! Me too! Me too! Me too!"

"O do be quiet, Chuggy!"

"Yes, close that big beak!"

Splash!

"What was that?"

"Chuggy, I think. Overboard I think. Dizzy is as dizzy does."

"The stars are on our side."

"What do you mean?"

"They dizzied Parrot overboard."

"They are winking at us," Musician agreed.

"Will we ever get to Island?"

"Oh yes," Musician said. "If there's no storm to blow us the other way, that's guaranteed."

"Let's not stay forever!"

"Just a visit to say hello," Musician said. "There are lots of islands to see. More islands than you can count."

"Do we visit them all!"

"O yes!"

"And the ocean goes on and on?"

"On and on."

"Let's have storms! Lots of storms! We need storms in order to blow us somewhere else and to blow parrots away. Not to us. One more will be two too many."

"Wind will make sure to blow some exciting storms," Musician said. And blow away someone's Snore Snore too, he thought.

"Yes, you can count on Wind to do something."

"Or nothing."

"Or nothing."

"Listen! Did you hear that?"

"Hear what?"

"Wet Chuggy! Wet Chuggy!"

"It sounds like a parrot coming out of the sea."

"A half-drowned parrot. Serves it right."

"Serves Chuggy right! Serves Chuggy right!"

The stars in the sky winked, winked, winked. And their pointed teeth spoke, "Shine some light right over there! Look, that boat is going to the island!"

"And that island is going to the boat."

"We shall show it the way."

"Can't miss it."

"That parrot learned a lesson."

"You think?"

"Let's stop spinning the world!"

"Look, they are asleep, asleep."

"Our turn to fun, fun, fun really!"

No one on the boat saw the stars whirling, exploding as they do at a star party. Not even Parrot, Chuggy by name, reacted with one eye open, one eye closed until one eye open looked at silver light bouncing off the waves and bouncing off what paddled over the waves. Too much party! Chuggy thought. Everyone is coming to the party! It had been a long time since Parrot had had a good squawk and Parrot would like the humans to wake up and give the name to these thousands and thousands of paddlers. So that Chuggy could say it, Chuggy could say the word he didn't know when they hopped on board. O well, "SQUAWK!" it squawked instead.

SQUAWK

"Musician!"

"That's me!" Musician awoke. "What is it, O one I sing to?"

"Frogs! An ocean of frogs from the big wave at the beginning of the story, I think they must come. A boat-load of frogs. Each one wanting a storybook kiss! Abandon the boat! You have a few pops of corn, have you? Without my mermaid tail, I won't get very far, and same for you."

"No, nothing to pop, not a one. Parrot took it all. The first step we take off the boat will be to go down, down."

Musician and Gariella exchanged a "What good are you?" look. And then some turtle talk came their way.

"Me? I here am. Excuse, can I help, me? Good very. I help can."

"Hello, Turtle!"

"Followed! Me the frogs followed, followed or I. Brought us Big Wave here! Nowhere of out! Back to island, climb up, all the way, swim and carry on my back you two, one and makes one two! So far, good so!"

"Is there a pillow?" asked Gariella.

"O, lean back on its head!"

"Turtle won't mind?"

"Mind? Don't my mind mind!"

"No, your head!"

"Head? Full speed, yes, it goes ahead! Island we go!"

If it's a question of nothing else to hop about on, frogs will settle for a boat as Parrot could see. Chuggy gave them every chance. Every chance to teach him what to say. "Croak croak croak. Croak croak croak." A lot of frog lips came Chuggy's way but no crackers, no tea. Nothing. Nothing but lips ready for a parrot kiss. "Croak! Croak!"

Maybe the time had come to kiss a bird and fly away from Boat. After all, hadn't a horse been one of them? If you can kiss a horse and gallop away as did Claudius the Fabulous, then try it on a bird if a kiss is all you've got to get out of an ocean everywhere and back to marsh sweet marsh!

"Not me!" Chuggy squawked, and flew from Boat. You never know which way a kiss will go. The last thing Chuggy wanted was to kiss a frog and, as a result, hop about with a croak, croak, croak. He made up this frightened song as he flew away:

Kiss a frog

croak, croak, croak

then a frog

Chuggy will be!

Or kiss, kiss, kiss

lots of frogs

and have me, me, me

drinking all the tea.

Too much company!
O, I think I will fly
and not hop hop hop
on a boat in the sea.

THE END

The author has written a number of novels for adults as well as a memoir of his friendship with the Canadian painter David Taylor. He is also a prolific children's story writer much due to his niece who inspired him one autumn leaf-strewn evening when she didn't want to be turned into a princess if caught by her pursuer. <u>Chase Me!</u> began it all.